GOING ON A LI...

HARRIET ZIEFERT AND MAVIS SMITH

PUFFIN BOOKS

I'm going on a lion hunt.

What's this? Quicksand?
Can't walk through it.

What's this?   A swamp?
Can't go around it.

Can't go through it.

Have to climb over it!

What's this?   A river?
Can't go over it.

Can't go under it.

Have to sail across it!

What's this? A cliff?
Can't go over it.

Can't go under it.

Have to slide down it!

What's this?
A herd of elephants?

Can't go around it.
Can't go through it.

Have to ride over it!

I hear a noise.
I think I've found the...

LION!

Have to run away from him!

Have to keep ahead of him!

Safe at last!